Mark Antony D. W. Howe

The Memory of Lincoln

Mark Antony D. W. Howe

The Memory of Lincoln

ISBN/EAN: 9783337092795

Printed in Europe, USA, Canada, Australia, Japan

Cover: Foto ©Raphael Reischuk / pixelio.de

More available books at **www.hansebooks.com**

THE
MEMORY OF LINCOLN

Poems · Selected
With an Introduction by
M. A. DeWolfe Howe

SCIRE

QVOD · SCIENDVM

Boston
Small Maynard & Company
1899

The Rockwell & Churchill Press
Boston, U.S.A.

Grateful acknowledgment is due to Mr. John James Piatt, Mr. Richard Henry Stoddard, Mr. Edmund Clarence Stedman, Mr. Richard Watson Gilder, Dr. S. Weir Mitchell, Mr. Maurice Thompson, Messrs. Houghton, Mifflin, & Co., Messrs. Charles Scribner's Sons, Mr. George Boker and The J. B. Lippincott Co., Messrs. Harper & Brothers, and The Century Co., for permission to reprint poems written or controlled through copyright by them. The publishers of Walt Whitman are the publishers of the present volume, for which, moreover, the poem by Mr. Paul Laurence Dunbar was written. Of Mr. R. H. Stoddard's sonnet, " Abraham Lincoln," the last two lines have been changed by the author for the republication of the poem in this place. The frontispiece of the volume is used through the courtesy of Messrs. A. W. Elson & Co., by whom the original picture is copyrighted.

The Editor would especially record his obligation to the New York State Library School at Albany for the use of an unpublished bibliography of poems relating to Lincoln — the work of Miss Mary L. Sutliff. Though the selections presented here are few, it is believed that by the aid of this bibliography the broad field from which they are taken has been entirely surveyed.

CONTENTS

Page

IX INTRODUCTION: *The Poetic Memory of Lincoln*
                                    The Editor

3 SONNET IN 1862   *John James Piatt*

4 From the ODE RECITED AT THE HARVARD COMMEMO—
  RATION   *James Russell Lowell*

7 O CAPTAIN! MY CAPTAIN   *Walt Whitman*

9 From AN HORATIAN ODE   *Richard Henry Stoddard*

12 ABRAHAM LINCOLN: Foully Assassinated, April 19, 1865
                                    Tom Taylor

16 From OUR HEROIC THEMES   *George Henry Boker*

18 From ABRAHAM LINCOLN   *Henry Howard Brownell*

35 THE MARTYR   *Herman Melville*

37 WHEN LILACS LAST IN THE DOORYARD BLOOM'D
                                    Walt Whitman

50 From the GETTYSBURG ODE   *Bayard Taylor*

52 ABRAHAM LINCOLN   *Richard Henry Stoddard*

53 THE EMANCIPATION GROUP   *John Greenleaf Whittier*

55 THE HAND OF LINCOLN   *Edmund Clarence Stedman*

58 ON THE LIFE—MASK OF ABRAHAM LINCOLN
                                  Richard Watson Gilder

59 TO THE SPIRIT OF ABRAHAM LINCOLN
                                  Richard Watson Gilder

60 LINCOLN   *S. Weir Mitchell*

61 From LINCOLN'S GRAVE   *Maurice Thompson*

65 LINCOLN   *Paul Laurence Dunbar*

THE POETIC MEMORY OF ABRAHAM LINCOLN.

The memory of Abraham Lincoln is preserved through the record of the impressions he made upon many minds representing many phases of thought and action in war and peace. Since this record deals in general with outward acts, it is well worth while to supplement it by a consideration of inward impulses. The outward act is but the flowering of a seed which lies within the soul. To this interior ground the poets guide our eyes, and what they reveal to us there explains everything. It is needed but to know truly the heart of a man in order to be sure of the words he will speak and the deeds he will perform when the occasion is ripe for speech and action.

In the fulness of poetic record providing such knowledge as this, Lincoln stands practically alone. Certainly his treatment at poetic hands is without parallel in American history. We turn to Washington for such a parallel, and, for various reasons, it does not exist. If it is not to be found there, where else shall we look ? It is not enough to say that Lincoln's time was preëminently the time of song, and that a thousand singers were ready at his death either to break their silence or to keep it unbroken. Nor can it be declared without reserve that the cause for which he died rendered him at the time necessarily " the sub-

[ix]

ject of all verse." An overflowing volume of " Poetical Tributes to the Memory of Abraham Lincoln," published in 1865, preserves the sorrowing chorus of the day. Its mightily preponderating note had the high virtue of sincerity, but lacked many others. Yet in that volume, and in the other writings which sprang less directly from the " sad occasion dear " of Lincoln's death, certain notes of true poetic quality are distinguishable. It is with these, more particularly when they do not express the immediate grief or the instinct to avenge the blackest of murders, but help us to see the true Lincoln, and to realize what his life has variously meant to men whose chief care is for the inmost things, — it is with these that our present concern lies.

There is no portion of Lowell's " Ode Recited at the Harvard Commemoration," in the summer of 1865, more justly familiar than the lines referring to Lincoln. These were not in the Ode as Lowell recited it, but were added immediately afterwards. It was inevitable that he should wish to leave in the finished poem some clear record of his feeling towards the central human figure of the events which called to the sons of Harvard to give their lives for their country. It was hardly less to be expected that, in celebrating the heroic gift in song, Lowell should look upon Lincoln just as he did. As one versed equally in the lore of books and of character peculiar to his native land, it was manifestly for him to compare and analyze, and as a total result of the process, to see and draw a poet's picture of the man in whom " nothing of Europe " might be found, — unless as in " one of Plutarch's men," —but instead a creature made of the

> ". . . sweet clay from the breast
> Of the unexhausted West."

The Lincoln of Lowell's far-flung vision was ultimately the " new birth of our new soil, the first American." And to somewhat the same purposes of acute analysis and definition Mr. R. H. Stoddard, in the lines from his noble " Horatian Ode," which have to do especially with Lincoln's character, has devoted the rarely combined powers of poet and critic.

It is, of course, for quite another view of Lincoln that we look to Walt Whitman. In the burning lines, " O Captain ! My Captain ! " which many readers consider Whitman's highest achievement, because, they would say, it is " least like him," the poet sings his loyalty and grief from the full heart and for the complete utterance of those who in one way and another fought by Lincoln's side. Whitman's own service in the hospitals brought home to him especially the significance of death by war. Therefore in the longer threnody for Lincoln, " When Lilacs Last in the Door-Yard Bloom'd," is it not surprising (it would be more surprising if Whitman were not the singer) that Lincoln himself is less the theme than " death, its thought, and the sacred knowledge of death." But Lincoln enters into the highly imagined chant more than as the mere cause for its being. Whitman, looking out upon " the large unconscious scenery " of his land, translates the meaning of Lincoln's name for him into terms of the democracy he is never weary of singing; and to adorn the chamber-walls of " the burial house of him " he loved, calls up

" Pictures of growing spring and farms and homes,"

and scenes from " the city at hand," from the crowded " life and the workshops," and from the whole " varied and ample land." Whitman thus speaks for many when he draws from the thought of Lincoln a multitude of images inherently American; and tenderly defining his " captain " as " the sweetest, wisest soul of all my days and lands," he makes his own offering of one of the single phrases by which it is easiest to remember Lincoln as he was.

While Whitman's fame increases, that of another true singer of Lincoln becomes unhappily less. This is Henry Howard Brownell, the poet whom Farragut called to serve on his staff before the battle of Mobile Bay, which thus secured the enduring poetic memorial of " The Bay Fight." Mr. Aldrich's sonnet in Brownell's praise describes him as one who

THE MEMORY OF LINCOLN

" . . . knew books, and hearts of men,
Cities and camps, and war's immortal woe."

It is therefore not the unexpected which happens when we find in Brownell's long and not too highly polished poem, "Abraham Lincoln," written in the summer of 1865, perhaps the truest blending of the civic and the martial aspects of Lincoln's character. When the mere President was his theme, Brownell, like Lowell and Mr. Stoddard, showed how well he knew the "hearts of men," at least the heart of the one man who was dearest to the nation. But the President, to him who saw actual service in the Civil War, was in a true sense also "Commander-in-Chief of the Army and Navy of the United States;" and Brownell, meditating on the dead leader, turned his thought back to the "Hartford" with its "long decks all slaughter-sprent," and thence naturally upward to the vision of the "lost battalions" drawn up in a celestial review, — "a grander Review than Grant's," — passing "in mighty square and column" before the ascended President. This is indeed one of the true poetic visions toward which few pages of American poetry have more directly opened the windows of the soul.

The statelier threnodies for Lincoln must not lead us to forget the very different memorial written by Tom Taylor for *Punch*. There is a value all its own

in this humble, generous recantation of the scoffer
who acknowledges that all scoffing has been due to
the imperfect vision which could not know at once what
truth and strength were hid beneath a forbidding sur-
face; and we cannot resent this "glittering chaplet
brought from other lands" as Alice Cary did when
she wrote :

> "What need hath he now of a tardy crown,
>   His name from mocking jest and sneer to save?
> When every ploughman turns his furrow down
>   As soft as though it fell upon his grave."

For our generation the beauty of the last two of
these lines, rather than the spirit of the first two, is the
memorable thing. For us, indeed, there is perhaps
even a greater present, if less poetic, interest in the
lines which Whittier, soon after the appearance of
Tom Taylor's verses, took occasion to copy from his
poem "To Englishmen" (1862), and sent with this
brief letter, printed in the "New York Times," of
June 5, 1865, to a Canadian correspondent:

AMESBURY, MASS., May 22, 1865.

MY DEAR SIR :

The tears which both nations are shedding over the
grave of our beloved President are washing out all
bitter memories of misconception and estrangement
between them. So good comes of evil.

[xiv]

THE MEMORY OF LINCOLN

O Englishmen ! in hope and creed,
   In blood and tongue our brothers ;
We too are heirs of Runnymede,
And Shakespeare's fame and Cromwell's deed
   Are not alone our mother's.

Thicker than water in one rill,
   Through centuries of story,
Our Saxon blood has flowed, and still
We share with you the good and ill,
   The shadow and the glory.
           Thine truly,
            JOHN G. WHITTIER.

If the wish to share in the established glory of Lincoln came promptly from our kinsmen across the seas, it has come no less positively, though of course more slowly, from our own countrymen of the South. The poem read by Mr. Maurice Thompson before the Harvard Phi Beta Kappa in 1893 speaks eloquently for the great change wrought by time ; for here the voice of one who in his own person fought against the Northern cause is uplifted in whole-souled praise of Lincoln's greatness. In the same year of 1893 the poems for the opening of the World's Columbian Exposition and for the unveiling of a Lincoln statue in Edinburgh to the memory of Scottish-American soldiers gave token of the living presence of Lincoln's spirit in regions so truly far apart as Illinois and Scotland. Such words about him as those which Mr. Paul Laurence Dunbar contributes to this volume were sure to come in time from one of Mr. Dunbar's race. The various separated songs, uttering each its particular note of response to Lincoln's appeal to the soul of man, might be counted to an amazing number. As if possibly to remind us that the least conventional of men had within him that symmetry of nature which is best interpreted by the most austere of poetical forms, these poems are cast with notable frequency in the mould of the sonnet. Through all the poems of which Mr. Stedman's " The Hand of Lincoln " and the sonnets of Dr. Mitchell and Mr. Gilder may be taken as types, the calmer American judgment of a long period of peace finds clear expression, and thus there is still a constant pledge that the cherishing of Lincoln's memory has become indeed a portion of our national heritage.

Fortunately we may not be expected to let slip even a little of our knowledge of Abraham Lincoln. But if upon the record by which he lives disaster could be conceived to fall with discriminating hand, destroying the libraries of prose, and leaving untouched the small body of the best verse which poets have made for his praise, our words might well be, " Tho' much is taken, much abides." There would

THE MEMORY OF LINCOLN

still be left to us the spiritual outlines for a great
portrait. These lines have been drawn by many
hands, guided by eyes accustomed to look for widely
varying symbols of character. Yet the complete
personality which they enable us to reconstruct has
none other than the unity, blending within itself all
human complexities of tenderness and strength, of the
very Lincoln we have come to know through the
cumulative testimony of a host of his fellow-men.

Bristol, Rhode Island,
  January, 1899.

[xvii]

THE MEMORY OF LINCOLN

JOHN JAMES PIATT

SONNET IN 1862

Stern be the Pilot in the dreadful hour
   When a great nation, like a ship at sea
   With the wroth breakers whitening at her lee,
Feels her last shudder if her Helmsman cower;
A godlike manhood be his mighty dower!
   Such and so gifted, Lincoln, may'st thou be
   With thy high wisdom's low simplicity
And awful tenderness of voted power:
From our hot records then thy name shall stand
   On Time's calm ledger out of passionate days —
With the pure debt of gratitude begun,
   And only paid in never-ending praise —
One of the many of a mighty Land,
Made by God's providence the Anointed One.

John James Piatt
 1862

[3]

THE MEMORY OF LINCOLN

From the

ODE RECITED AT THE HARVARD COMMEMORATION

Life may be given in many ways,
And loyalty to Truth be sealed
As bravely in the closet as the field,
   So bountiful is Fate ;
   But then to stand beside her,
   When craven churls deride her,
To front a lie in arms and not to yield,
   This shows, methinks, God's plan
   And measure of a stalwart man,
   Limbed like the old heroic breeds,
   Who stand self-poised on manhood's solid earth,
 Not forced to frame excuses for his birth,
Fed from within with all the strength he needs.

Such was he, our Martyr-Chief
   Whom late the Nation he had led,
   With ashes on her head,
Wept with the passion of an angry grief :
Forgive me, if from present things I turn
To speak what in my heart will beat and burn,
And hang my wreath on his world-honored urn.
   Nature, they say, doth dote,
   And cannot make a man
   Save on some worn-out plan,

[4]

Repeating us by rote :
For him her Old World moulds aside she threw,
    And, choosing sweet clay from the breast
    Of the unexhausted West,
With stuff untainted shaped a hero new,
Wise, steadfast in the strength of God, and true.
    How beautiful to see
Once more a shepherd of mankind indeed,
Who loved his charge, but never loved to lead ;
One whose meek flock the people joyed to be,
    Not lured by any cheat of birth,
    But by his clear-grained human worth,
And brave old wisdom of sincerity !
    They knew that outward grace is dust ;
    They could not choose but trust
In that sure-footed mind's unfaltering skill,
    And supple-tempered will
That bent like perfect steel to spring again and thrust.
    His was no lonely mountain-peak of mind,
    Thrusting to thin air o'er our cloudy bars,
    A sea-mark now, now lost in vapors blind ;
    Broad prairie rather, genial, level-lined,
    Fruitful and friendly for all human kind,
Yet also nigh to heaven and loved of loftiest stars.
    Nothing of Europe here,
Or, then, of Europe fronting mornward still,
    Ere any names of Serf and Peer
    Could Nature's equal scheme deface

[5]

THE MEMORY OF LINCOLN

And thwart her genial will;
Here was a type of the true elder race,
And one of Plutarch's men taiked with us face to face.
I praise him not; it were too late;
And some innative weakness there must be
In him who condescends to victory
Such as the Present gives, and cannot wait,
Safe in himself as in a fate.
So always firmly he:
He knew to bide his time,
And can his fame abide,
Still patient in his simple faith sublime,
Till the wise years decide.
Great captains, with their guns and drums,
Disturb our judgment for the hour,
But at last silence comes;
These all are gone, and, standing like a tower,
Our children shall behold his fame.
The kindly-earnest, brave, foreseeing man,
Sagacious, patient, dreading praise, not blame,
New birth of our new soil, the first American.

James Russell Lowell
    1865

*By special permission of
    Messrs. Houghton, Mifflin & Co.*

O CAPTAIN! MY CAPTAIN

O Captain! my Captain! our fearful trip is done,
The ship has weather'd every rack, the prize we
    sought is won,
The port is near, the bells I hear, the people all
    exulting,
While follow eyes the steady keel, the vessel grim and
    daring;
        But O heart! heart! heart!
          O the bleeding drops of red,
            Where on the deck my Captain lies,
            Fallen cold and dead.

O Captain! my Captain! rise up and hear the bells;
Rise up — for you the flag is flung — for you the
    bugle trills,
For you bouquets and ribbon'd wreaths — for you the
    shores a-crowding,
For you they call, the swaying mass, their eager faces
    turning;
        Here Captain! dear father!
          This arm beneath your head!
           It is some dream that on the deck,
           You've fallen cold and dead.

My Captain does not answer, his lips are pale and
    still,

[7]

THE MEMORY OF LINCOLN

My father does not feel my arm, he has no pulse nor
    will,
The ship is anchor'd safe and sound, its voyage closed
    and done,
From fearful trip the victor ship comes in with object
    won;

Exult O shores, and ring O bells!
But I with mournful tread,
Walk the deck my Captain lies,
Fallen, cold and dead.

Walt Whitman
1865

RICHARD HENRY STODDARD

From

AN HORATIAN ODE

Cool should be, of balanced powers,
The ruler of a race like ours,
    Impatient, headstrong, wild, —
    The man to guide the child!

And this he was, who most unfit
(So hard the sense of God to hit!)
    Did seem to fill his place.
    With such a homely face, —

Such rustic manners, — speech uncouth, —
(That somehow blundered out the truth!)
    Untried, untrained to bear
    ·The more than kingly care!

Ay! and his genius put to scorn
The proudest in the purple born,
    Whose wisdom never grew
    To what, untaught, he knew —

The people, of whom he was one.
No gentleman like Washington, —
    (Whose bones, methinks, make room,
    To have him in their tomb!)

[9]

THE MEMORY OF LINCOLN

A laboring man, with horny hands,
Who swung the axe, who tilled his lands,
    Who shrank from nothing new,
    But did as poor men do!

One of the people!   Born to be
Their curious epitome;
    To share, yet rise above
    Their shifting hate and love.

Common his mind (it seemed so then),
His thoughts the thoughts of other men :
    Plain were his words, and poor —
    But now they will endure!

No hasty fool, of stubborn will,
But prudent, cautious, pliant, still;
    Who, since his work was good,
    Would do it, as he could.

Doubting, was not ashamed to doubt,
And, lacking prescience, went without :
    Often appeared to halt,
    And was, of course, at fault :

Heard all opinions, nothing loth,
And loving both sides, angered both :
    Was — not like justice, blind,
    But watchful, clement, kind.

RICHARD HENRY STODDARD

No hero this, of Roman mould;
Nor like our stately sires of old :
    Perhaps he was not great —
    But he preserved the State !

O honest face, which all men knew !
O tender heart, but known to few !
    O wonder of the age,
    Cut off by tragic rage !

Richard Henry Stoddard
1865

*By special permission of
Messrs. Charles Scribner's Sons.*

ABRAHAM LINCOLN

FOULLY ASSASSINATED, APRIL 14, 1865

You lay a wreath on murdered Lincoln's bier!
   You, who with mocking pencil wont to trace,
Broad for the self-complacent British sneer,
   His length of shambling limb, his furrowed face,

His gaunt, gnarled hands, his unkempt, bristling hair,
   His garb uncouth, his bearing ill at ease,
His lack of all we prize as debonair,
   Of power or will to shine, of art to please;

You, whose smart pen backed up the pencil's laugh,
   Judging each step, as though the way were plain;
Reckless, so it could point its paragraph,
   Of chief's perplexity, or people's pain!

Beside this corpse, that bears for winding-sheet
   The stars and stripes he lived to rear anew,
Between the mourners at his head and feet,
   Say, scurrile jester, is there room for *you?*

Yes; he had liv'd to shame me from my sneer,
   To lame my pencil, and confute my pen,
To make me own this hind of princes peer,
   This rail-splitter a true-born king of men.

[12]

My shallow judgment I had learn'd to rue,
   Noting how to occasion's height he rose;
How his quaint wit made home-truth seem more true;
   How, iron-like, his temper grew by blows;

How humble, yet how hopeful he could be;
   How in good fortune and in ill the same;
Nor bitter in success, nor boastful he,
   Thirsty for gold, nor feverish for fame.

He went about his work, — such work as few
   Ever had laid on head and heart and hand, —
As one who knows, where there's a task to do,
   Man's honest will must Heaven's good grace com-
      mand;

Who trusts the strength will with the burden grow,
   That God makes instruments to work his will,
If but that will we can arrive to know,
   Nor tamper with the weights of good and ill.

So he went forth to battle, on the side
   That he felt clear was Liberty's and Right's,
As in his peasant boyhood he had plied
   His warfare with rude Nature's thwarting mights, —

The unclear'd forest, the unbroken soil,
   The iron bark that turns the lumberer's axe,
The rapid that o'erbears the boatman's toil,
   The prairie hiding the maz'd wanderer's tracks,

[13]

THE MEMORY OF LINCOLN

The ambush'd Indian, and the prowling bear, —
    Such were the deeds that help'd his youth to train :
Rough culture, but such trees large fruit may bear,
    If but their stocks be of right girth and grain.

So he grew up, a destin'd work to do,
    And liv'd to do it ; four long-suffering years'
Ill fate, ill feeling, ill report, liv'd through,
    And then he heard the hisses change to cheers,

The taunts to tribute, the abuse to praise,
    And took both with the same unwavering mood, —
Till, as he came on light from darkling days,
    And seem'd to touch the goal from where he stood,

A felon hand, between the goal and him,
    Reach'd from behind his back, a trigger prest —
And those perplex'd and patient eyes were dim,
    Those gaunt, long-laboring limbs were laid to rest.

The words of mercy were upon his lips,
    Forgiveness in his heart and on his pen,
When this vile murderer brought swift eclipse
    To thoughts of peace on earth, goodwill to men.

The Old World and the New, from sea to sea,
    Utter one voice of sympathy and shame.
Sore heart, so stopped when it at last beat high !
    Sad life, cut short just as its triumph came !

[14]

TOM TAYLOR

A deed accurs'd! Strokes have been struck before
   By the assassin's hand, whereof men doubt
If more of horror or disgrace they bore;
   But thy foul crime, like Cain's, stands darkly out,

Vile hand, that brandest murder on a strife,
   Whate'er its grounds, stoutly and nobly striven,
And with the martyr's crown crownest a life
   With much to praise, little to be forgiven.

Tom Taylor
  Punch, *London, May 6, 1865*

THE MEMORY OF LINCOLN

From

OUR HEROIC THEMES

(READ BEFORE THE PHI BETA KAPPA SOCIETY OF
HARVARD UNIVERSITY.)

Crown we our heroes with a holier wreath
Than man e'er wore upon this side of death ;
Mix with their laurels deathless asphodels,
And chime their pæans from the sacred bells !
Nor in your prayers forget the martyred Chief,
Fallen for the gospel of your own belief,
Who, ere he mounted to the people's throne,
Asked for your prayers, and joined in them his own.
I knew the man.   I see him, as he stands
With gifts of mercy in his outstretched hands ;
A kindly light within his gentle eyes,
Sad as the toil in which his heart grew wise ;
His lips half-parted with the constant smile
That kindled truth, but foiled the deepest guile ;
His head bent forward, and his willing ear
Divinely patient right and wrong to hear :
Great in his goodness, humble in his state,
Firm in his purpose, yet not passionate,
He led his people with a tender hand,
And won by love a sway beyond command,
Summoned by lot to mitigate a time
Frenzied with rage, unscrupulous with crime,
He bore his mission with so meek a heart

GEORGE HENRY BOKER

That Heaven itself took up his people's part;
And when he faltered, helped him ere he fell,
Eking his efforts out by miracle.
No king this man, by grace of God's intent;
No, something better, freeman, — President!
A nature, modeled on a higher plan,
Lord of himself, an inborn gentleman!

George Henry Boker
1865

*By special permission of the
J. B. Lippincott Co.*

THE MEMORY OF LINCOLN

From

ABRAHAM LINCOLN

Dead is the roll of the drums,
   And the distant thunders die,
   They fade in the far-off sky;
And a lovely summer comes,
   Like the smile of Him on high.

Lulled, the storm and the onset.
   Earth lies in a sunny swoon;
   Stiller splendor of noon,
Softer glory of sunset,
   Milder starlight and moon!

For the kindly Seasons love us;
   They smile over trench and clod
(Where we left the bravest of us,) —
   There's a brighter green of the sod,
And a holier calm above us
   In the blesséd Blue of God.

The roar and ravage were vain;
   And Nature, that never yields,
Is busy with sun and rain
At her old sweet work again
   On the lonely battle-fields.

How the tall white daisies grow,
   Where the grim artillery rolled !
(Was it only a moon ago ?
   It seems a century old,) —

And the bee hums in the clover,
   As the pleasant June comes on ;
Aye, the wars are all over, —
   But our good Father is gone.

There was tumbling of traitor fort,
   Flaming of traitor fleet —
Lighting of city and port,
   Clasping in square and street.

There was thunder of mine and gun,
   Cheering by mast and tent, —
When — his dread work all done,
And his high fame full won —
   Died the Good President.

In his quiet chair he sate,
   Pure of malice or guile,
Stainless of fear or hate, —
   And there played a pleasant smile
On the rough and careworn face ;
   For his heart was all the while
On means of mercy and grace.

[19]

THE MEMORY OF LINCOLN

The brave old Flag drooped o'er him,
  (A fold in the hard hand lay,) —
  He looked, perchance, on the play, —
But the scene was a shadow before him,
  For his thoughts were far away.

'Twas but the morn, (yon fearful
  Death-shade, gloomy and vast,
  Lifting slowly at last,)
  His household heard him say,
" 'Tis long since I've been so cheerful,
  So light of heart as to-day."

'Twas dying, the long dread clang, —
  But, or ever the blessèd ray
  Of peace could brighten to day,
  Murder stood by the way —
Treason struck home his fang!
One throb — and, without a pang,
  That pure soul passed away.

    .   .   .   .   .   .

Kindly Spirit! — Ah, when did treason
  Bid such a generous nature cease,
Mild by temper and strong by reason,
  But ever leaning to love and peace?

HENRY HOWARD BROWNELL

A head how sober; a heart how spacious;
 A manner equal with high or low;
Rough but gentle, uncouth but gracious,
 And still inclining to lips of woe.

Patient when saddest, calm when sternest,
 Grieved when rigid for justice' sake;
Given to jest, yet ever in earnest
 If aught of right or truth were at stake.

Simple of heart, yet shrewd therewith,
 Slow to resolve, but firm to hold;
Still with parable and with myth
 Seasoning truth, like Them of old;
Aptest humor and quaintest pith!
 (Still we smile o'er the tales he told.)

. . . . . .

Yet whoso might pierce the guise
 Of mirth in the man we mourn,
Would mark, and with grieved surprise,
 All the great soul had borne,
In the piteous lines, and the kind, sad eyes
 So dreadfully wearied and worn.

And we trusted (the last dread page
 Once turned, of our Dooms-day Scroll,)
 To have seen him, sunny of soul,
In a cheery, grand old age.

[21]

THE MEMORY OF LINCOLN

But, Father, 'tis well with thee!
  And since ever, when God draws nigh,
Some grief for the good must be,
  'Twas well, even so to die, —

'Mid the thunder of Treason's fall,
  The yielding of haughty town,
The crashing of cruel wall,
  The trembling of tyrant crown!

The ringing of hearth and pavement
  To the clash of falling chains, —
The centuries of enslavement
  Dead, with their blood-bought gains!

And through trouble weary and long,
  Well hadst thou seen the way,
Leaving the State so strong
  It did not reel for a day;

And even in death couldst give
  A token for Freedom's strife —
A proof how republics live,
  And not by a single life,

But the Right Divine of man,
  And the many, trained to be free, —
And none, since the world began,
  Ever was mourned like thee.

[22]

HENRY HOWARD BROWNELL

Dost thou feel it, O noble Heart !
  (So grieved and so wronged below,)
From the rest wherein thou art ?
Do they see it, those patient eyes ?
Is there heed in the happy skies
  For tokens of world-wide woe ?

The Land's great lamentations,
  The mighty mourning of cannon,
    The myriad flags half-mast —
The late remorse of the nations,
  Grief from Volga to Shannon !
    (Now they know thee at last.)

How, from gray Niagara's shore
  To Canaveral's surfy shoal —
From the rough Atlantic roar
  To the long Pacific roll —
  For bereavement and for dole,
Every cottage wears its weed,
  White as thine own pure soul,
And black as the traitor deed. .

How, under a nation's pall,
  The dust so dear in our sight
    To its home on the prairie past, —
The leagues of funeral,
  The myriads, morn and night,
    Pressing to look their last.

[23]

THE MEMORY OF LINCOLN

Nor alone the State's Eclipse;
  But tears in hard eyes gather —
And on rough and bearded lips,
Of the regiments and the ships —
  " Oh, our dear Father!"

And methinks of all the million
  That looked on the dark dead face,
'Neath its sable-plumed pavilion,
  The crone of a humbler race
Is saddest of all to think on,
  And the old swart lips that said,
Sobbing, " Abraham Lincoln!
  Oh, he is dead, he is dead!"

Hush! let our heavy souls
  To-day be glad; for agen
The stormy music swells and rolls,
  Stirring the hearts of men.

And under the Nation's Dome,
  They've guarded so well and long,
Our boys come marching home,
  Two hundred thousand strong.

All in the pleasant month of May,
  With war-worn colors and drums,
Still through the livelong summer's day,
  Regiment, regiment comes.

HENRY HOWARD BROWNELL

Like the tide, yesty and barmy,
  That sets on a wild lee-shore,
Surge the ranks of an army
  Never reviewed before!

Who shall look on the like agen,
  Or see such host of the brave?
A mighty River of marching men
  Rolls the Capital through —
Rank on rank, and wave on wave,
  Of bayonet-crested blue!

How the chargers neigh and champ,
(Their riders weary of camp,)
  With curvet and with caracole! —
The cavalry comes with thundrous tramp,
  And the cannons heavily roll.

And ever, flowery and gay,
The Staff sweeps on in a spray
  Of tossing forelocks and manes;
But each bridle-arm has a weed
Of funeral, black as the steed
  That fiery Sheridan reins.

Grandest of mortal sights
  The sun-browned ranks to view —
The Colors ragg'd in a hundred fights,
  And the dusty Frocks of Blue!

[25]

And all day, mile on mile,
With cheer, and waving, and smile,
The war-worn legions defile
   Where the nation's noblest stand;
And the Great Lieutenant looks on,
   With the Flower of a rescued Land, —
For the terrible work is done,
And the Good Fight is won
   For God and for Fatherland.

So, from the fields they win,
   Our men are marching home,
   A million are marching home!
To the cannon's thundering din,
   And banners on mast and dome, —
And the ships come sailing in
With all their ensigns dight,
As erst for a great sea-fight.

Let every color fly,
   Every pennon flaunt in pride;
Wave, Starry Flag, on high!
Float in the sunny sky,
   Stream o'er the stormy tide!
For every stripe of stainless hue,
And every star in the field of blue,
Ten thousand of the brave and true
   Have laid them down and died.

And in all our pride to-day
  We think, with a tender pain,
Of those so far away
  They will not come home again.

And our boys had fondly thought,
  To-day, in marching by,
From the ground so dearly bought,
And the fields so bravely fought,
  To have met their Father's eye.

But they may not see him in place,
  Nor their ranks be seen of him;
We look for the well-known face,
  And the splendor is strangely dim.

Perished? — who was it said
  Our Leader had passed away?
Dead?   Our President dead?
  He has not died for a day!

We mourn for a little breath
  Such as, late or soon, dust yields;
But the Dark Flower of Death
  Blooms in the fadeless fields.

We looked on a cold, still brow,
  But Lincoln could yet survive;
  He never was more alive,
Never nearer than now.

[27]

THE MEMORY OF LINCOLN

For the pleasant season found him,
  Guarded by faithful hands,
  In the fairest of Summer Lands;
With his own brave Staff around him,
  There our President stands.

There they are all at his side,
  The noble hearts and true,
  That did all men might do —
Then slept, with their swords, and died.

    .   .   .   .   .   .

And around — (for there can cease
  This earthly trouble) — they throng,
The friends that have passed in peace,
  The foes that have seen their wrong.

(But, a little from the rest,
  With sad eyes looking down,
  And brows of softened frown,
With stern arms on the chest,
Are two, standing abreast —
  Stonewall and Old John Brown.)

But the stainless and the true,
  These by their President stand,
To look on his last review,
  Or march with the old command.

[28]

HENRY HOWARD BROWNELL

And lo ! from a thousand fields,
   From all the old battle-haunts,
A greater Army than Sherman wields,
   A grander Review than Grant's !

Gathered home from the grave,
   Risen from sun and rain —
Rescued from wind and wave
   Out of the stormy main —
The Legions of our Brave
   Are all in their lines again !

Many a stout Corps that went,
Full-ranked, from camp and tent,
   And brought back a brigade ;
Many a brave regiment,
   That mustered only a squad.

The lost battalions,
   That, when the fight went wrong,
Stood and died at their guns, —
   The stormers steady and strong,

With their best blood that bought
   Scarp, and ravelin, and wall, —
The companies that fought
   Till a corporal's guard was all.

[29]

Many a valiant crew,
　That passed in battle and wreck, —
Ah, so faithful and true!
　They died on the bloody deck,
They sank in the soundless blue.

All the loyal and bold
　That lay on a soldier's bier, —
　The stretchers borne to the rear,
The hammocks lowered to the hold.

The shattered wreck we hurried,
　In death-fight, from deck and port, —
The Blacks that Wagner buried —
　That died in the Bloody Fort!

Comrades of camp and mess,
　Left, as they lay, to die,
In the battle's sorest stress,
　When the storm of fight swept by, —
They lay in the Wilderness,
　Ah, where did they not lie?

In the tangled swamp they lay,
　They lay so still on the sward! —
They rolled in the sick-bay,
Moaning their lives away —
　They flushed in the fevered ward.

They rotted in Libby yonder,
    They starved in the foul stockade —
Hearing afar the thunder
    Of the Union cannonade !

But the old wounds all are healed,
    And the dungeoned limbs are free, —
The Blue Frocks rise from the field,
    The Blue Jackets out of the sea.

They've 'scaped from the torture-den,
    They've broken the bloody sod,
They're all come to life agen ! —
The Third of a Million men
    That died for Thee and for God !

A tenderer green than May
    The Eternal Season wears, —
The blue of our summer's day
    Is dim and pallid to theirs, —
The Horror faded away,
    And 'twas heaven all unawares !

Tents on the Infinite Shore !
    Flags in the azuline sky,
Sails on the seas once more !
    To-day, in the heaven on high,
All under arms once more !

[31]

THE MEMORY OF LINCOLN

The troops are all in their lines,
   The guidons flutter and play;
But every bayonet shines,
   For all must march to-day.

What lofty pennons flaunt?
What mighty echoes haunt,
   As of great guns, o'er the main?
   Hark to the sound again —
The Congress is all a-taunt!
   The Cumberland's manned again!

Ail the ships and their men
   Are in iine of battle to-day, —
All at quarters, as when
   Their last roll thundered away, —
All at their guns, as then,
   For the Fleet salutes to-day.

The armies have broken camp
   On the vast and sunny plain,
   The drums are rolling again;
With steady, measured tramp,
   They're marching all again.

With alignment firm and solemn,
   Once again they form
In mighty square and column, —
   But never for charge and storm.

The Old Flag they died under
  Floats above them on the shore,
And on the great ships yonder
  The ensigns dip once more —
And once again the thunder
  Of the thirty guns and four!

In solid platoons of steel,
  Under heaven's triumphal arch,
The long lines break and wheel —
  And the word is, " Forward, march!"

The Colors ripple o'erhead,
  The drums roll up to the sky,
And with martial time and tread
  The regiments all pass by —
The ranks of our faithful Dead,
  Meeting their President's eye.

With a soldier's quiet pride
  They smile o'er the perished pain,
  For their anguish was not vain —
For thee, O Father, we died!
  And we did not die in vain.

March on, your last brave mile!
  Salute him, Star and Lace,
Form round him, rank and file,
  And look on the kind, rough face;

[33]

THE MEMORY OF LINCOLN

But the quaint and homely smile
    Has a glory and a grace
It never had known erewhile —
    Never, in time and space.

Close round him, hearts of pride !
Press near him, side by side, —
    Our Father is not alone !
For the Holy Right ye died,
And Christ, the Crucified,
    Waits to welcome His own.

Henry Howard Brownell.
    1865

HERMAN MELVILLE

THE MARTYR

INDICATIVE OF THE PASSION OF THE PEOPLE ON THE
15TH OF APRIL, 1865

Good Friday was the day
　Of the prodigy and crime,
When they killed him in his pity,
　When they killed him in his prime
Of clemency and calm —
　When with yearning he was filled
　To redeem the evil-willed,
And, though conqueror, be kind;
　　But they killed him in his kindness,
　　In their madness and their blindness,
And they killed him from behind.

　　There is sobbing of the strong,
　　　And a pall upon the land;
　　But the People in their weeping　·
　　　Bare the iron hand:
　　Beware the People weeping
　　　When they bare the iron hand.

He lieth in his blood —
　The father in his face;
They have killed him, the Forgiver —
　The Avenger takes his place,

[35]

THE MEMORY OF LINCOLN

The Avenger wisely stern,
   Who in righteousness shall do
   What the heavens call him to,
And the parricides remand;
   For they killed him in his kindness,
   In their madness and their blindness,
And his blood is on their hand.

There is sobbing of the strong,
   And a pall upon the land;
But the People in their weeping
   Bare the iron hand:
Beware the People weeping
   When they bare the iron hand.

Herman Melville.
1865.

By special permission of
   Messrs. Harper & Brothers.

[36]

WHEN LILACS LAST IN THE DOORYARD BLOOM'D.

1

When lilacs last in the dooryard bloom'd,
And the great star early droop'd in the western sky
in the night,
I mourn'd, and yet shall mourn with ever-returning
spring.

Ever-returning spring, trinity sure to me you bring,
Lilac blooming perennial and drooping star in the
west,
And thought of him I love.

2

O powerful western fallen star!
O shades of night — O moody, tearful night!
O great star disappear'd — O the black murk that
hides the star!
O cruel hands that hold me powerless — O helpless
soul of me!
O harsh surrounding cloud that will not free my soul.

3

In the dooryard fronting an old farm-house near the
white-wash'd palings,
Stands the lilac-bush tall-growing with heart-shaped
leaves of rich green,

[37]

With many a pointed blossom rising delicate, with
    the perfume strong I love,
With every leaf a miracle — and from this bush in
    the dooryard,
With delicate-color'd blossoms and heart-shaped leaves
    of rich green,
A sprig with its flower I break.

4

In the swamp in secluded recesses,
A shy and hidden bird is warbling a song.

Solitary the thrush,
The hermit withdrawn to himself, avoiding the settle-
    ments,
Sings by himself a song.

Song of the bleeding throat,
Death's outlet song of life, (for well dear brother I
    know,
If thou wast not granted to sing thou would'st surely
    die.)

5

Over the breast of the spring, the land, amid cities,
Amid lanes and through old woods, where lately the
    violets peep'd from the ground, spotting the
    gray debris,

Amid the grass in the fields each side of the lanes,
    passing the endless grass,
Passing the yellow-spear'd wheat, every grain from
    its shroud in the dark-brown fields uprisen,
Passing the apple-tree blows of white and pink in the
    orchards,
Carrying a corpse to where it shall rest in the grave,
Night and day journeys a coffin.

6

Coffin that passes through lanes and streets,
Through day and night with the great cloud darken-
    ing the land,
With the pomp of the inloop'd flags with the cities
    draped in black,
With the show of the States themselves as of crape-
    veil'd women standing,
With processions long and winding and the flambeaus
    of the night,
With the countless torches lit, with the silent sea of
    faces and the unbared heads,
With the waiting depot, the arriving coffin, and the
    sombre faces,
With the dirges through the night, with the thousand
    voices rising strong and solemn,
With all the mournful voices of the dirges pour'd
    around the coffin,

[39]

The dim-lit churches and the shuddering organs —
  where amid these you journey,
With the tolling tolling bell's perpetual clang,
Here, coffin that slowly passes,
I give you my sprig of lilac.

7

(Nor for you, for one alone,
Blossoms and branches green to coffins all I bring,
For fresh as the morning, thus would I chant a song
  for you O sane and sacred death.

All over bouquets of roses,
O death, I cover you over with roses and early lilies,
But mostly and now the lilac that blooms the first,
Copious I break, I break the sprigs from the bushes,
With loaded arms I come, pouring for you,
For you and the coffins all of you O death !)

8

O western orb sailing the heaven,
Now I know what you must have meant as a month
  since I walk'd,
As I walk'd in silence the transparent shadowy night,
As I saw you had something to tell as you bent to me
  night after night,
As you dropp'd from the sky low down as if to my
  side, (while the other stars all look'd on,)

As we wander'd together the solemn night, (for something I know not what kept me from sleep,)
As the night advanced, and I saw on the rim of the
  west how full you were of woe,
As I stood on the rising ground in the breeze in the
  cool transparent night,
As I watch'd where you pass'd and was lost in the
  netherward black of the night,
As my soul in its trouble dissatisfied sank, as where
  you sad orb,
Concluded, dropt in the night, and was gone.

9

Sing on there in the swamp,
O singer bashful and tender, I hear your notes, I
  hear your call,
I hear, I come presently, I understand you,
But a moment I linger, for the lustrous star has
  detain'd me,
The star my departing comrade holds and detains me.

10

O how shall I warble myself for the dead one there I
  loved?
And how shall I deck my song for the large sweet
  soul that has gone?
And what shall my perfume be for the grave of him I
  love?

[41]

THE MEMORY OF LINCOLN

Sea-winds blown from east and west,
Blown from the Eastern sea and blown from the
    Western sea, till there on the prairies meeting,
These and with these and the breath of my chant,
I'll perfume the grave of him I love.

II

O what shall I hang on the chamber walls?
And what shall the pictures be that I hang on the
    walls,
To adorn the burial-house of him I love?

Pictures of growing spring and farms and homes,
With the Fourth-month eve at sundown, and the gray
    smoke lucid and bright,
With floods of the yellow gold of the gorgeous, indo-
    lent, sinking sun, burning, expanding the air,
With the fresh sweet herbage under foot, and the
    pale green leaves of the trees prolific,
In the distance the flowing glaze, the breast of the
    river, with a wind-dapple here and there,
With ranging hills on the banks, with many a line
    against the sky, and shadows,
And the city at hand with dwellings so dense, and
    stacks of chimneys,
And all the scenes of life and the workshops, and the
    workmen homeward returning.

12

Lo, body and soul — this land,
My own Manhattan with spires, and the sparkling and
　　hurrying tides, and the ships,
The varied and ample land, the South and the North
　　in the light, Ohio's shores and flashing Missouri,
And ever the far-spreading prairies cover'd with grass
　　and corn.

Lo, the most excellent sun so calm and haughty,
The violet and purple morn with just-felt breezes,
The gentle soft-born measureless light,
The miracle spreading bathing all, the fulfill'd noon,
The coming eve delicious, the welcome night and the
　　stars,
Over my cities shining all, enveloping man and land.

13

Sing on, sing on you gray-brown bird,
Sing from the swamps, the recesses, pour your chant
　　from the bushes,
Limitless out of the dusk, out of the cedars and pines.

Sing on, dearest brother, warble your reedy song,
Loud human song, with voice of uttermost woe.

O liquid and free and ténder!
O wild and loose to my soul — O wondrous singer!

[43]

You only I hear — yet the star holds me, (but will
    soon depart,)
Yet the lilac with mastering odor holds me.

14

Now while I sat in the day and look'd forth,
In the close of the day with its light and the fields of
    spring, and the farmers preparing their crops,
In the large unconcious scenery of my land with its
    lakes and forests,
In the heavenly aerial beauty, (after the perturb'd
    winds and the storms,)
Under the arching heavens of the afternoon swift
    passing, and the voices of children and women,
The many moving sea-tides, and I saw the ships how
    they sail'd,
And the summer approaching with richness, and the
    fields all busy with labor,
And the infinite separate houses, how they all went
    on, each with its meals and minutia of daily
    usages,
And the streets how their throbbings throbb'd, and the
    cities pent — lo, then and there,
Falling upon them all, and among them all, envelop-
    ing me with the rest,
Appear'd the cloud, appear'd the long, black trail,
And I knew death, its thought, and the sacred knowl-
    edge of death.

Then with the knowledge of death as walking one
　　side of me,
And the thought of death close-walking the other side
　　of me,
And I in the middle as with companions, and as hold-
　　ing the hands of companions,
I fled forth to the hiding receiving night that talks not,
Down to the shores of the water, the path by the
　　swamp in the dimness,
To the solemn shadowy cedars and ghostly pines so
　　still.

And the singer so shy to the rest receiv'd me,
The gray-brown bird I know receiv'd us comrades
　　three,
And he sang the carol of death, and a verse for him I
　　love.

From deep secluded recesses,
From the fragrant cedars and the ghostly pines so
　　still,
Came the carol of the bird.

And the charm of the carol rapt me,　　　　　　 .
As I held as if by their hands my comrades in the
　　night,
And the voice of my spirit tallied the song of the
　　bird.

[45]

THE MEMORY OF LINCOLN

Come lovely and soothing death,
Undulate round the world, serenely arriving, arriving,
In the day, in the night, to all, to each,
Sooner or later delicate death.

Prais'd be the fathomless universe,
For life and joy, and for objects and knowledge curious,
And for love, sweet love — but praise! praise! praise!
For the sure-enwinding arms of cool-enfolding death.

Dark mother always gliding near with soft feet,
Have none chanted for thee a chant of fullest welcome?
Then I chant it for thee, I glorify thee above all,
I bring thee a song that when thou must indeed come,
      come unfalteringly.

Approach strong deliveress,
When it is so, when thou hast taken them I joyously sing
      the dead,
Lost in the loving floating ocean of thee,
Laved in the flood of thy bliss O death.

From me to thee glad serenades,
Dances for thee I propose saluting thee, adornments and
      feastings for thee,
And the sights of the open landscape and the high-spread
      sky are fitting,
And life and the fields, and the huge and thoughtful
      night.

The night in silence under many a star,
The ocean shore and the husky whispering wave whose
     voice I know,
And the soul turning to thee O vast and well-veil'd death,
And the body gratefully nestling close to thee.

Over the tree-tops I float thee a song,
Over the rising and sinking waves, over the myriad
     fields and the prairies wide,
Over the dense-pack'd cities all and the teeming wharves
     and ways,
I float this carol with joy, with joy to thee O death.

15

To the tally of my soul,
Loud and strong kept up the gray-brown bird,
With pure deliberate notes spreading filling the night.

Loud in the pines and cedars dim,
Clear in the freshness moist and the swamp-perfume,
And I with my comrades there in the night.

While my sight that was bound in my eyes unclosed,
As to long panoramas of visions.

And I saw askant the armies,
I saw as in noiseless dreams hundreds of battle-flags,
Borne through the smoke of the battles and pierc'd
     with missiles I saw them,

And carried hither and yon through the smoke, and
    torn and bloody,
And at last but a few shreds left on the staffs, (and
    all in silence,)
And the staffs all splinter'd and broken.

I saw battle-corpses, myriads of them,
And the white skeletons of young men, I saw them,
I saw the debris and debris of all the slain soldiers of
    the war,
But I saw they were not as was thought,
They themselves were fully at rest, they suffer'd not,
The living remain'd and suffer'd, the mother suffer'd,
And the wife and the child and the musing comrade
    suffer'd,
And the armies that remain'd suffered.

16

Passing the visions, passing the night,
Passing, unloosing the hold of my comrades' hands,
Passing the song of the hermit bird and the tallying
    song of my soul,
Victorious song, death's outlet song, yet varying ever-
    altering song,
As low and wailing, yet clear the notes, rising and
    falling, flooding the night,
Sadly sinking and fainting, as warning and warning,
    and yet again bursting with joy,

[48]

Covering the earth and filling the spread of the heaven,
As that powerful psalm in the night I heard from
      recesses,
Passing, I leave thee lilac with heart-shaped leaves,
I leave thee there in the door-yard, blooming, re-
      turning with spring.

I cease from my song for thee,
From my gaze on thee in the west, fronting the west,
      communing with thee,
O comrade lustrous with silver face in the night.

Yet each to keep and all, retrievements out of the night,
The song, the wondrous chant of the gray-brown bird,
And the tallying chant, the echo arous'd in my soul,
With the lustrous and drooping star with the counte-
      nance full of woe,
With the holders holding my hand nearing the call
      of the bird,
Comrades mine and I in the midst, and their memory
      ever to keep, for the dead I loved so well,
For the sweetest, wisest soul of all my days and lands
      — and this for his dear sake,
Lilac and star and bird twined with the chant of my
      soul,
There in the fragrant pines and the cedars dusk and dim.

Walt Whitman.
1865.

THE MEMORY OF LINCOLN

From the

GETTYSBURG ODE

DEDICATION OF THE NATIONAL MONUMENT

After the eyes that looked, the lips that spake
Here, from the shadows of impending death,
    Those words of solemn breath,
    What voice may fitly break
The silence, doubly hallowed, left by him ?
We can but bow the head, with eyes grown dim,
    And, as a Nation's litany, repeat
The phrase his martyrdom hath made complete,
Noble as then, but now more sadly sweet :
" Let us, the Living, rather dedicate
Ourselves to the unfinished work, which they
Thus far advanced so nobly on its way,
    And saved the perilled State !
Let us, upon this field where they, the brave,
Their last full measure of devotion gave,
Highly resolve they have not died in vain ! —
That, under God, the Nation's later birth
    Of Freedom, and the people's gain
Of their own Sovereignty, shall never wane
And perish from the circle of the earth ! "
From such a perfect text, shall Song aspire
    To light her faded fire,
    And into wandering music turn
Its virtue, simple, sorrowful, and stern ?

BAYARD TAYLOR

His voice all elegies anticipated;
    For, whatsoe'er the strain,
    We hear that one refrain :
" We consecrate ourselves to them, the Con-
    secrated ! "

Bayard Taylor.
   1869.

By special permission of
   Messrs. Houghton, Mifflin & Co.

ABRAHAM LINCOLN

This man whose homely face you look upon
Was one of Nature's masterful, great men;
Born with strong arms, that unfought battles won,
Direct of speech and cunning with the pen.
Chosen for large designs, he had the art
Of winning with his humor, and he went
Straight to his mark, which was the human heart;
Wise, too, for what he could not break, he bent.
Upon his back a more than Atlas-load,
The burden of the Commonwealth, was laid;
He stooped, and rose up to it, though the road
Shot suddenly downward, not a whit dismayed:
Patiently resolute, what the stern hour
Demanded, that he was, — that Man, that Power.

Richard Henry Stoddard.
1877.

By special permission of
Messrs. Charles Scribner's Sons.

JOHN GREENLEAF WHITTIER

THE EMANCIPATION GROUP

(PARK SQUARE, BOSTON; DUPLICATE OF THE FREED-
MEN'S MEMORIAL STATUE, LINCOLN SQUARE, WASH-
INGTON)

Amidst thy sacred effigies
　　Of old renown give place,
O city, Fredom-loved! to his
　　Whose hand unchained a race.

Take the worn frame, that rested not
　　Save in a martyr's grave;
The care-lined face, that none forgot,
　　Bent to the kneeling slave.

Let man be free!　The mighty word
　　He spoke was not his own;
An impulse from the Highest stirred
　　These chiselled lips alone.

The cloudy sign, the fiery guide,
　　Along his pathway ran,
And Nature, through his voice, denied
　　The ownership of man.

We rest in peace where these sad eyes
　　Saw peril, strife, and pain;
His was the nation's sacrifice,
　　And ours the priceless gain.

[53]

THE MEMORY OF LINCOLN

O symbol of God's will on earth
  As it is done above !
Bear witness to the cost and worth
  Of justice and of love.

Stand in thy place and testify
  To coming ages long,
That truth is stronger than a lie,
  And righteousness than wrong.

John Greenleaf Whittier.
1879.

By special permission of
  Messrs. Houghton, Mifflin & Co.

EDMUND CLARENCE STEDMAN

THE HAND OF LINCOLN

Look on this cast, and know the hand
　That bore a nation in its hold :
From this mute witness understand
　What Lincoln was, — how large of mould

The man who sped the woodman's team,
　And deepest sunk the ploughman's share,
And pushed the laden raft astream,
　Of fate before him unaware.

This was the hand that knew to swing
　The axe — since thus would Freedom train
Her son — and made the forest ring,
　And drove the wedge, and toiled amain.

Firm hand, that loftier office took,
　A conscious leader's will obeyed,
And, when men sought his word and look,
　With steadfast might the gathering swayed.

No courtier's, toying with a sword,
　Nor minstrel's, laid across a lute ;
A chief's, uplifted to the Lord
　When all the kings of earth were mute !

[55]

THE MEMORY OF LINCOLN

The hand of Anak, sinewed strong,
   The fingers that on greatness clutch;
Yet lo! the marks their lines along
   Of one who strove and suffered much.

For here in knotted cord and vein
   I trace the varying chart of years;
I know the troubled heart, the strain,
   The weight of Atlas — and the tears.

Again I see the patient brow
   That palm erewhile was wont to press;
And now 'tis furrowed deep, and now
   Made smooth with hope and tenderness.

For something of a formless grace
   This moulded outline plays about;
A pitying flame, beyond our trace,
   Breathes like a spirit, in and out, —

The love that cast an aureole
   Round one who, longer to endure,
Called mirth to ease his ceaseless dole,
   Yet kept his nobler purpose sure.

Lo, as I gaze, the statured man,
   Built up from yon large hand, appears:
A type that Nature wills to plan
   But once in all a people's years.

[56]

EDMUND CLARENCE STEDMAN

What better than this voiceless cast
　To tell of such a one as he,
Since through its living semblance passed
　The thought that bade a race be free!

Edmund Clarence Stedman.
　1883.

By special permission of
　Messrs. Houghton, Mifflin & Co.

ON THE LIFE–MASK OF ABRAHAM LINCOLN

This bronze doth keep the very form and mold
  Of our great martyr's face.   Yes, this is he :
  That brow all wisdom, all benignity ;
  That human, humorous mouth ; those cheeks that
      hold
Like some harsh landscape all the summer's gold ;
  That spirit fit for sorrow, as the sea
  For storms to beat on ; the lone agony
  Those silent, patient lips too well foretold.
Yes, this is he who ruled a world of men
  As might some prophet of the elder day —
  Brooding above the tempest and the fray
With deep-eyed thought and more than mortal ken.
  A power was his beyond the touch of art
  Or armèd strength — his pure and mighty heart.

Richard Watson Gilder.
  1886.

By special permission of
  The Century Co.

RICHARD WATSON GILDER

TO THE SPIRIT OF ABRAHAM LINCOLN

(REUNION AT GETTYSBURG TWENTY–FIVE YEARS AFTER THE BATTLE)

Shade of our greatest, O look down to-day !
   Here the long, dread midsummer battle roared,
   And brother in brother plunged the accursèd
      sword ; —
   Here foe meets foe once more in proud array
Yet not as once to harry and to slay
   But to strike hands, and with sublime accord
   Weep tears heroic for the souls that soared
   Quick from earth's carnage to the starry way.
Each fought for what he deemed the people's good,
   And proved his bravery with his offered life,
   And sealed his honor with his outpoured blood ;
But the Eternal did direct the strife,
   And on this sacred field one patriot host
   Now calls thee father, — dear, majestic ghost !

Richard Watson Gilder.
   1888.

By special permission of
The Century Co.

LINCOLN

Chained by stern duty to the rock of state,
  His spirit armed in mail of rugged mirth,
  Ever above, though ever near to earth,
  Yet felt his heart the cruel tongues that sate
Base appetites, and foul with slander, wait
  Till the keen lightnings bring the awful hour
  When wounds and suffering shall give them power.
  Most was he like to Luther, gay and great,
Solemn and mirthful, strong of heart and limb.
  Tender and simple too; he was so near
  To all things human that he cast out fear,
And, ever simpler, like a little child,
  Lived in unconscious nearness unto Him
  Who always on earth's little ones hath smiled.

S. *Weir Mitchell.*
  1891.

By special permission of
  The Century Co.

MAURICE THOMPSON

From

LINCOLN'S GRAVE

(READ BEFORE THE PHI BETA KAPPA SOCIETY OF
HARVARD UNIVERSITY)

May one who fought in honor for the South
Uncovered stand and sing by Lincoln's grave?
Why, if I shrunk not at the cannon's mouth,
Nor swerved one inch for any battle-wave,
Should I now tremble in this quiet close,
Hearing the prairie wind go lightly by
From billowy plains of grass and miles of corn,
  While out of deep repose
The great sweet spirit lifts itself on high
And broods above our land this summer morn?

 . . . .

Meseems I feel his presence. Is he dead?
Death is a word. He lives and grander grows.
At Gettysburg he bows his bleeding head;
He spreads his arms where Chickamauga flows,
As if to clasp old soldiers to his breast,
Of South or North no matter which they be,
Not thinking of what uniform they wore,
  His heart a palimpsest,
Record on record of humanity,
Where love is first and last forevermore.

 . . . .

THE MEMORY OF LINCOLN

He was the Southern mother leaning forth,
At dead of night to hear the cannon roar,
Beseeching God to turn the cruel North
And break it that her son might come once more;
He was New England's maiden pale and pure,
Whose gallant lover fell on Shiloh's plain;
He was the mangled body of the dead;
  He writhing did endure
Wounds and disfigurement and racking pain,
Gangrene and amputation, all things dread.

He was the North, the South, the East, the West,
The thrall, the master, all of us in one;
There was no section that he held the best;
His love shone as impartial as the sun;
And so revenge appealed to him in vain,
He smiled at it, as at a thing forlorn,
And gently put it from him, rose and stood
  A moment's space in pain,
Remembering the prairies and the corn
And the glad voices of the field and wood.

 . . . .

And then when Peace set wing upon the wind
And northward flying fanned the clouds away,
He passed as martyrs pass. Ah, who shall find
The chord to sound the pathos of that day!
Mid-April blowing sweet across the land,
New bloom of freedom opening to the world,

MAURICE THOMPSON

Loud pæans of the homeward-looking host,
　　The salutations grand
From grimy guns, the tattered flags upfurled;
And he must sleep to all the glory lost!

Sleep! loss!　But there is neither sleep nor loss,
And all the glory mantles him about;
Above his breast the precious banners cross,
Does he not hear his armies tramp and shout?
Oh, every kiss of mother, wife or maid
Dashed on the grizzly lip of veteran,
Comes forthright to that calm and quiet mouth,
　　And will not be delayed,
And every slave, no longer slave but man,
Sends up a blessing from the broken South.
　　　.　　.　　.　　.　　.　　.　　.　.

He is not dead, France knows he is not dead;
He stirs strong hearts in Spain and Germany,
In far Siberian mines his words are said,
He tells the English Ireland shall be free,
He calls poor serfs about him in the night,
And whispers of a power that laughs at kings,
And of a force that breaks the strongest chain;
　　Old tyranny feels his might
Tearing away its deepest fastenings,
And jewelled sceptres threaten him in vain.

Years pass away, but freedom does not pass,
Thrones crumble, but man's birthright crumbles not,

[63]

THE MEMORY OF LINCOLN

And, like the wind across the prairie grass,
A whole world's aspirations fan this spot
With ceaseless panting after liberty,
One breath of which would make dark Russia fair,
And blow sweet summer through the exile's cave,
    And set the exile free;
For which I pray, here in the open air
Of Freedom's morning-tide, by Lincoln's grave.

Maurice Thompson
    1893.

PAUL LAURENCE DUNBAR

LINCOLN

Hurt was the Nation with a mighty wound,
And all her ways were filled with clam'rous sound.
Wailed loud the South with unremitting grief,
And wept the North that could not find relief.
Then madness joined its harshest tone to strife:
A minor note swelled in the song of life
Till, stirring with the love that filled his breast,
But still, unflinching at the Right's behest
Grave Lincoln came, strong-handed, from afar, —
The mighty Homer of the lyre of war!
'Twas he who bade the raging tempest cease,
Wrenched from his strings the harmony of peace,
Muted the strings that made the discord, — Wrong,
And gave his spirit up in thund'rous song.
Oh, mighty Master of the mighty lyre!
Earth heard and trembled at thy strains of fire:
Earth learned of thee what Heav'n already knew,
And wrote thee down among her treasured few!

Paul Laurence Dunbar
    1899.